OGRES
DO DISCO

For Louie;
happiness is being who you are

OGRES
DO DISCO

KIRSTY MCKAY

Illustrated by Chris Judge

Andersen Press

First published in 2016 by
Andersen Press Limited
20 Vauxhall Bridge Road
London SW1V 2SA
www.andersenpress.co.uk

2 4 6 8 10 9 7 5 3 1

British Library Cataloguing in Publication Data available.

ISBN 978 1 78344 296 6

Printed and bound in Great Britain
by CPI Group UK (Ltd), Croydon CR0 4YY

There is a magical land, far, far away. The sky is cornflower blue, with white clouds like whippy cream. The mountains are the deepest purple, capped with shimmering sugar-icing snow. The valley is green with trees, and sprinkled with beautiful, fragrant flowers of every colour. The sun shines, a warm breeze blows, and birds sing sweetly. This magical land is snoozy and calm. This magical land is peaceful.

But not today.

'Ogden! Caaaaaaaaaatch!'

Ogden the ogre looked up and saw a

1

huge fishing net on a stick flying through the air towards him.

'Grab it, Ogden!' Willow, his best friend, screamed again. She jumped up and down on the spot. **'Caaatch!'**

The net was high in the sky, but Ogden was very tall, and very nimble.

He could do this! He bent his knobbly knees and leaped up into the air.

His two left feet were pointing and his glittering pink wellies sparkling in the light.

'Got it, Little Will!' he cried to his friend.

Reaching out with a long, green, warty arm he caught the net and landed with a thud on the soft grass.

'Look out, Ogden!' Willow pointed. 'The ratties are escaping!'

Ogden looked around, and sure enough, a dozen black, hairy creatures were scampering over the clearing towards the woods. They had long, furry bodies and skinny, pink legs. They moved quickly. Too quickly.

'Stop, you Squeaky Ratifers!' Ogden bellowed.

They didn't hear him. The Ratifers were small, but they were louder than Ogden and Willow put together, which is very loud indeed. Nothing squeaks as loudly as a Squeaky Ratifer. Imagine nine hundred and ninety-nine mice swinging on a rusty gate, and you haven't even come close to how loudly a Ratifer can squeak.

Ogden watched the Ratifers run about and rubbed his green face. If the ratties got to the trees they'd be lost in the thick undergrowth. He didn't have any time to lose. Ogden stretched out his long ogre legs and bounded after them, the ground thudding beneath him. With a swift **sweeeeep** of the net, he caught three ratties at once. Another scoop, and he'd snatched two more.

'Go, Og!' Willow shouted.

Swipe!

Ogden bagged another Ratifer, then another. They squeaked all the more loudly, and wriggled in the net, their bony legs kicking, long, whiskery noses twitching and sharp, pointy teeth gnawing at the net. But they were stuck fast.

Ogden fixed his eyes on the last three Squeaky Ratifers. They were the biggest of the bunch and the fastest too. And they were nearly at the trees, with only brave Willow in their way.

'Come and get your breakfast, ratties!' Willow stood firm. She rolled a huge wicker basket onto its side, and flipped the lid open.

Ogden grinned a big grin, guessing her plan. But at the last moment the three Ratifers changed direction and made a dash towards the Sinky-Stinky Bog. Ogden scratched his head. Surely they weren't going to swim for it? He straightened up to his full height. If they did try to escape, he was ready for them. The Sinky-Stinky Bog held no fear for him – he had his rhinestone-encrusted wellies on, after all. He dunked the net into the wicker basket, depositing the other Ratifers.

SLAM!

Willow shut the lid as Ogden turned and faced the final three ratties, who had come to a halt at the edge of the bog.

Ogden tiptoed towards them.

'Nowhere to run, Ratifers!' he said to them. 'Nowhere to hide!'

He held out the net, and the Ratifers gnashed their teeth. Ogden was not afraid. He took a step forward, and held the net up high, preparing to swipe. But just as he was about to make his move—

'Yeah! Yeah! Yeeeeah!
Dooo the Funky Chicken!'

A blast of music rang out from the woods. Ogden turned to look.

'Dooooo, doooo, doooo,
do the Funky, Funky Chicken!'

'Happy sounds?' Ogden said, dropping the net. His knobbly knees bent, and his big behind started to sway in time with the jumpety-bumpety music.

'Og, no!' Willow cried. 'The Ratifers are getting away!'

Ogden turned back to where the Ratifers had been cowering in front of the bog. They weren't there any more. They had dodged around him and were scampering off into the woods.

'Come back, you tricksy ratties!' Ogden roared, and made a dash for it. But he had forgotten the net on the ground. As he tried to run he tripped over the net and barrelled into Willow and the wicker basket.

'Whoooooooops!'

Ogden and Willow fell onto their

behinds at the corner of the Sinky-Stinky
Bog, sending big, dirty splashes of gooey,
pooey mud into the air.

splaaaaaat!

The mud landed on their heads.
'The basket!' cried Willow.

'Them ratties!' cried Ogden.

But it was too late. They turned to see the basket rolling away and the lid falling open. One by one, the captured Ratifers leaped out to freedom, and scrambled full pelt into the woods.

'Uh-oh!' said Ogden.

'Uh-oh is right,' Willow said, wiping mud from her face. 'We've lost them.'

'Them be back eating the villagers' foods again tonight.' Ogden sighed. 'Now Mayorman not trusts Og. Won't be big Guard Ogre at the jail any mores.' His lower lip wobbled.

'Nonsense!' Willow patted Ogden on the back with a muddy hand. 'Remember our motto? "We never give up!"' She reached and pulled him to his feet. 'We've come a long way since we first met, Ogden.

You used to be a man-eating monster with two left feet, but now look at you! Prize-winning ballroom dancer! Respected Guard Ogre, in charge of the village jail! And together, we're the brave Monster Masher Detectives.' She squeezed his big, warty hand. 'Ever since we outsmarted those scary Fluffy Grocklers and rescued the cobbler's triplet babies, the villagers have been depending on us to keep the valley monster-free. We'll catch those fiendish ratties, sure enough. Don't be blue.'

Ogden smiled a crinkly smile. 'Og not blue. Og green.'

'Oh, Ogden.' Willow laughed. 'You're a mean, green, dancing machine, all right. Just don't get distracted by that disco music next time.'

Ogden nodded, and dusted himself

down. 'The music is so
very jumpety-bumpety,
though, Little Will.'
He winked at her.
'Make Og want to
shake and shimmy.'

'Disco fever is contagious, it's true,'
said Willow, packing up the things and
leading Ogden to the path through the
woods. 'We're not far from the village hall,
so that must have been the band practising
for the Big Disco Night tomorrow. We'll
get a chance to show our new dancing
skills to the whole of the valley. But first
we have some monster-catching to do,
Detective Ogden.'

Ogden nodded, following Willow.
Soon they had reached a sunny clearing
in the woods. A mighty, knobbly oak tree

stood in the middle of the clearing, and in its branches nestled a tree house. This was Willow's home, but now it was also something else. A large sign was hanging from one of the boughs of the tree, and it swayed gently in the breeze. Rainbow-coloured glittery letters spelled out:

+THE MONSTER MASHERS'+
DETECTIVE
AGENCY
(NO PROBLEM TOO BEASTLY)

The two friends climbed wearily up the ladder, and through the trapdoor.

'Now,' said Willow. 'A wash, a cup of elderberry tea, and then we'll make some ratty-catching plans.'

Ogden nodded, and plonked his plump backside onto a big beanbag.

Suddenly, there was a

crash-bang-wallop!

from somewhere below the tree house.

Something was down there.

Ogden and Willow peered over the tree-house railing, down to the clearing below. A rustling sound came from the undergrowth at the edge of the woods.

'Carefully-careful, Little Will!' Ogden warned, and the two of them ducked down behind a branch.

As they watched, the bushes parted, and a tall lady stumbled towards them. Her face was hidden by a huge, black, floppy hat. She had lanky legs clad in spotty purple satin, and two arms that clasped a bulging suitcase in front. She puffed and

panted as she staggered across the grass, crushing daisies under gold platform boots.

Ogden stood up, the hackles on his neck rising. 'A witch?' he whispered to Willow. 'Come to cast a dizzy spell on us?'

The lady in the clearing dropped the suitcase, and whipped off her hat, revealing a ruddy face and a tower of pink hair that stood up from her head like candyfloss.

'Where you at, treacle-tart?' she shouted. 'Phew! I'm hotter than a pair of hot pants!'

'Granny!' yelled Willow, jumping up and down on the spot.

'Willowtree!' The lady spotted her and waved, her sequined blouse shimmering in the sun. 'Come to Grandma!' She held out her arms, and Willow raced down the ladder into the clearing.

Ogden watched as Willow and the strange lady hugged. He slowly followed Willow down to the ground.

'But what a surprise, you're here a day early!' Willow said. 'Ogden.' She turned to her friend and beamed. 'This is my granny.'

The lady with the pink hair stomped over to Ogden. She was almost as tall as him in her platform boots.

'Hello, Granny,' Ogden said, holding out his gnarly hand for her to shake.

'The name's Jiggy, ogre,' the lady said. 'Gimme five!' She slapped hands high in the air with Ogden. 'Groovy. So you're the ogre I've heard about, the one with all the moves?' She jiggled a little. 'We'll see about that. Willow tells me you're great at the cha-cha!' She skittered across the grass in front of him. 'But I'm here to train you to D-I-S-C-O.'

Ogden frowned a crumply frown.

'Disco, Ogden!' Willow laughed.

'Og loves jumpety-bumpety dancing!' Ogden's face stretched into a toothy grin. 'Jiggy teach us more?'

'You got it.' Jiggy smiled back.

Willow jumped up and down, excitedly.

'I thought we could do with a little help before the Big Disco Night tomorrow. Granny Jiggy is the best disco dancer this side of the Purple Mountains.'

'Are you crazy, child?' Jiggy stuck a hand on one hip. 'Best this side of the Purple Mountains? Oh no-no.' She waggled a finger at Willow. 'Best in the whole kingdom, sweet pea!'

Willow giggled, and bent down beside Jiggy's suitcase. 'Granny!' she shouted, excitedly. 'You brought your glitter ball!' She stood up, a large, silver ball in her hands. 'It's beautiful!'

Ogden stared at the ball. As Willow held it, it seemed to wink at him. It was covered with lots of tiny little mirrors,

each one catching the light and sending rainbows dancing over the clearing.

'Boogaloo! Boogaloo!' Jiggy sang, doing a funny dance, her top half moving one way, her bottom half the other. 'Crazy legs! Get your disco feet moving to the **Boogaloo,** Ogden!'

'Og like the glittery ball,' he purred. 'But Og don't need to go to the booger loo.'

'No, Ogden!' Willow roared with laughter. 'The Electric **Boogaloo** is a special kind of disco dance. And Granny Jiggy is here to teach it to us.' She pointed to the suitcase. 'Ooh, Jiggy, you've even brought your boom box!'

'Of course I have!' Jiggy grinned at her. 'I never go anywhere without it!'

'Boom?' Ogden crinkled his brow, creeping towards the suitcase. 'The box goes . . . boom?'

'Plain to see, honeybee!' Jiggy skipped towards the suitcase, pulled out a long, silver box with black circles on either end. 'Or should I say, plain to hear.' She flicked a switch on the top of the box:

Wacka-wacka woo-woo!
Boogawooga, boogawooga!
Wham! Bam! Bam!

The jumpiest, bumpiest music sounds filled the clearing. As Ogden listened, a wiggly feeling started in his tummy, travelled up his back and down his arms, making him want to click his warty fingers. The beat from the boom box thumped through the earth, tingling Ogden's legs and making him want to shake his ogre hips.

He started to move, shuffling his feet and waving his hands in the air. There really was no avoiding disco fever.

'This ogre's on fire! You got the groove, my man!' Jiggy batted her long, glittery eyelashes at Ogden. She looked at Willow. 'Let's see what you can do, little Boo!'

Willow giggled, grabbing Ogden's hand and twirling him around, and then Jiggy took Willow's hand and led them both in a whirling dance across the clearing. As the music sped up, they found themselves at the foot of the ladder up to the tree house. 'Follow me!' Jiggy cried, climbing up the ladder, all the time still dancing. The others followed, copying her moves. They danced all through the tree house – past the hammock where Willow slept, past the big beanbag where Ogden liked to sit, past the wooden trunk where they kept all their dancing costumes, then back out onto the deck, boogying in the dappled sun.

When the music finally stopped, all three collapsed in an exhausted heap on the floor, panting and laughing.

'Og likes disco fever!' Ogden chortled.

'It sure is catching!' laughed Jiggy. 'Once the beat gets under your skin, you can never stop dancing!' She looked at Ogden and Willow. 'Talking of skin, what's that muck all over you? Boy oh boy, do you two stink!'

Willow shook her head. 'We were chasing Squeaky Ratifers and fell into the Sinky-Stinky Bog,' she explained.

'Rati-whats?' said Jiggy. 'Poo-ey!'

'We need to clean ourselves up, I know,' Willow said, standing up and looking at her mud-splattered clothes. 'Let's set to it, Ogden! Tomorrow's going to be busy. Ratifers to catch, new costumes to try on, and disco trophies to win.' She walked to the ladder and stifled a yawn. 'Ogden, can you help me get Jiggy's things into the tree house before I fall asleep?'

But Ogden didn't reply.

'Ogden?' Willow turned to where her ogre pal was resting on the beanbag.

'Snoooooore!'

'Uh-oh.' Jiggy winked at Willow. 'Looks like it's you and me, Willowtree. That ogre is dancing in slumberland. It sure is hard work being a disco-dancing Monster Masher!' **Zzzzz!**

The next morning Willow awoke bright and early. She jumped out of her hammock and sniffed the air. It was the day of the Big Disco Night! Soon her aunt Fenella would be here with their costumes.

Aunty Fenella had a clothes shop in the village. She always made the very best dance clothes in the valley – even special, glittery shoes for Ogden's two left feet. Ogden liked to wear brightly coloured, twirly dresses sprinkled with sequins and feathers. Willow loved to dance in a smart top hat and tails. Fenella had never made them disco clothes before, so Willow was excited to see what she would bring.

But for now, the sparkles would have to wait. First came the hard work of being detectives, and catching Ratifers. Willow pulled on her denim dungarees and laced up her running shoes. Whatever happened today, there would definitely be some running involved.

Jiggy was asleep, snoring lightly from a comfy mattress on the floor. Just as Willow was about to wake her, she heard a loud, squeaking noise. She tiptoed quickly to the deck railing and looked into the clearing below.

'Morning, Willowtree.' Jiggy sleepily shuffled up to the railing beside her. She yawned a big yawn. 'What's going down?'

Odgen appeared out of the trees,

dragging the huge wicker basket. The squeaking sound was coming from the basket.

'Uh-oh,' said Jiggy. 'Something tells me that's not a picnic.'

'No!' said Willow. 'It's much, much better!' She ran to the ladder and skibbled down the rungs. 'Ogden!' she shouted. 'Is that what I think it is?'

Ogden hauled the basket to the grassy knoll and sat down, heavily. He was as mucky as a piggy in a poke hole.

'You caught the Ratifers?'

Ogden nodded, and glumly held up his left-left foot. 'Og lost a sparkly welly.'

'We'll get you another, you clever thing.' Willow arrived beside him, and was about to pat him on the back, when she suddenly stopped. 'Poo-ey!' She clapped a hand over her mouth and nose. 'More mud, Ogden?'

'Yowza!' Jiggy jiggled up to them. 'Send in the suds, let's get the bath a-running for this grubster!' She held her nose delicately.

'Og swam the Sinky-Stinky Bog,' Ogden panted. 'Ratifers think they can hides under the crusty, fusty mud.' He rubbed a yucky hand over his forehead. 'They can'ts.'

The lid of the basket lifted up a little, and a long, hairy nose sniffled out. Ogden thumped his bare left-left foot on the lid and the nose squeaked and disappeared into the basket again.

'Ogden wake up in the nighttime, for to catch them ratties. So, so snoozy.' He leaned back onto the soft grass and closed his eyes. 'Maybe time for sleepy wink-winks now.'

'Og, you're a hero, that's for sure!' Willow cried. 'But you can't sleep now.' She tugged at his big, green hand. 'We have to practise for the Big Disco – tonight's the night.'

'Og wants shut-eye,' moaned Ogden. He closed his eyes and let out a little snore.

'No! You mustn't sleep!' Willow tickled him under the chin, but he didn't move.

'Wake up!' She waggled his warty nose, but he only snored all the more loudly. 'Get on your feet, dancer!' But Ogden just snorted and rolled over.

**Bam! Wham! A-boogalooga woo!
Bam! Wham! A-boogalooga woo!**

Willow looked up. Jiggy was standing by the boom box.

'Jumpety-bumpety?' Og muttered, his eyelids flickering.

**Wacka-wacka woo-woo!
Booga-booga-loo!**

'Must dance . . .' Ogden rose up from the grass, as if in a trance. His eyes were still closed, but he shuffled his two left feet in time to the music.

Willow's jaw dropped. 'Granny, it's working! He's waking up!'

Ogden began to move faster, shrugging his shoulders, nodding his head and spinning on the spot.

'Shake those hips, sugar-lips!' shouted Jiggy, turning up the volume.

'Mmm, sugar,' said Ogden, his eyes opening. 'Yum, yum.'

Jiggy held the glitter ball and spun it in the air. Ogden blinked at it. The glitter ball twinkled in the morning sun, sending little rainbow lights flying through the clearing.

'Don't stop now!' said Willow, taking Ogden's hand and swinging him around. 'You've got to stay awake!'

'Looks like I'm just in time,' Fenella called from the path to the village. Her cheeks were bright red and her curly hair was stuck to her forehead. 'Mama Jiggy! I thought you must be here. How are you?'

'Peachy keen, my baby girl!' shouted Jiggy, waving.

'Better than me, Mama, you betcha!' Fenella said, her hands on her knees. 'I've dragged this trunk of clothes all the way from my shop. Give me a hand, Ogden?'

'Sparkle disco costumes!' Ogden exclaimed gleefully and bounded over to Fenella. He picked up the big, wooden trunk as if it weighed nothing at all. He carried it and set it down in the middle of the clearing beside the wicker basket full of Ratifers. Sitting on the basket, he leaned over the costume trunk and flung open the lid.

'Not so fast, ogre!' Fenella shouted, and bustled up to him. 'You'll only make a mess.' She pulled him up off the basket.

'Cor, you're a pongy one, and no mistake! Go and have a splash in the stream and get all that muck off you.'

'It's all right, Og,' said Willow. 'We won't begin until you're back.'

Ogden tramped through the trees and found the babbling brook. The water was cool and clear, and he waded up to his knees and washed the Sinky-Stinky Bog off his body. 'All clean, and ready for sparkles!' He murmured to himself.

As Ogden splashed back to the riverbank, he thought he heard a strange noise. He stopped, and listened.

'Gobble-gobble-gobble.'

Ogden put his head on one side. Strange. That was nothing he had ever heard before. He decided to answer back.

'Gobble, gobble?' he called, looking

upstream, then downstream. A fish jumped, and a pretty butterfly fluttered by. But there was nothing unusual around. 'Gobble?' Ogden shrugged. Perhaps it had just been the water making an odd sound as it ran over the rocks. 'Og want to gobble,' he grumbled, rubbing his belly as he set off back to the tree house. 'Hungry tum.'

'Ah, Ogden,' Fenella said, as he came into the clearing. 'Now stand over there – and you too, Willow – and I will show you what I have made for you.'

Ogden and Willow stood side by side and bolt upright, as straight as soldiers standing to attention. They could hardly wait to see the costumes.

'That's better,' Fenella said. She turned to the trunk of goodies. 'Now, first – Willow.' She carefully unfolded a pair of

trousers made of the shiniest, pale blue satin, and held them up for all to see.

'Check out those threads!' Jiggy said. 'Try 'em on, Willowtree.'

Willow didn't need telling twice. She wriggled into the stretchy trousers, and tried out a few dance moves. She shook and waggled, and bent low, then jumped up again. As she turned from side to side, the trousers changed colour from blue into a shimmering light purple.

'Ooh!' Willow said, looking down at her legs. 'They look magical!'

'Made with the finest iridescent satin,' said Fenella, proudly. 'And to match . . .' She picked up a floaty top made in the same icy blue and shimmering purple colours. It was dotted with tiny silver sequins that winked in the sun, and as she held the top

up, its big sleeves
billowed in the
gentle breeze.
It almost looked
like it was flying.

'You'll look like a
boombastic butterfly!' Jiggy said, clapping
her hands. Willow slipped into the top and
started to dance. As she flung her arms
in the air it was true, the sleeves did look
like wings. Finally, Fenella gave her a
glittery pair of silver, lace-up shoes to
complete the outfit.

'We'll plait your hair in lots of little
braids,' Fenella said, delving into the trunk
once more and bringing out a glass jar of
little, round, twinkling things of
blue, purple and silver. 'See these
beads? We'll thread them onto

each braid. You'll certainly have the disco look.' She shut the trunk and started to brush Willow's long hair.

'Wow!' Willow said. 'I'm so excited!' She turned to Ogden. 'What do you think, Og? Isn't my costume amazing?'

Ogden looked at the ground, and sniffed. 'Nothing for big, green ogre.'

Fenella turned to him, and rolled her eyes. 'Oh, Ogden! Do you really think I'd forget about you?' She walked up to the trunk again. 'I've saved the best until last, you betcha!' She turned to open the trunk, still looking at Ogden, but instead of the costume trunk, her hands found the lid of the wicker basket. It was the one that had the Squeaky Ratifers inside. Before she realised what she was doing, she began to open it—

'Squeeeeeeek!' 'Squeeeeeek!' 'Squeeeeeeeeeeek!'

Ratty noses poked out of the top of the basket, and little pink feet scratched away at the opening.

'No, Aunty!' Willow shouted. Fenella squealed and fell over backwards. The Ratifers saw their chance and tried to squeeze out from under the lid – they were nearly free!

'Ogden!' shouted Willow. 'Do something!'

As the Ratifers pushed with their noses and scrabbled with their claws, Ogden only had a split second to think. He launched himself into the air, arms outstretched, desperately grabbing for the basket . . .

Ogden landed belly-first on top of the basket, with a huge **Crrrunch!** The lid closed, the Ratifers squeaked in fury, and Ogden sighed a big pheeeeew-eeee in relief.

'That was a close one!' Willow wiped her brow. 'Are you hurt, Aunty?'

'I'm tougher than I look.' Fenella picked herself up, shook grass out of her ginger curls and brushed leaves off her behind. 'What on earth have you got in that basket?' Willow opened her mouth to answer, but Fenella held up her hands to stop her speaking. 'On second thoughts,

I don't want to know.' She looked at Ogden. 'How many times have I told you to clear your monsters up after you?' Ogden hung his head. 'Now put them away properly, and then we'll dress you up.'

'The ratties should be somewhere safe for now. The jail?' Willow said, putting her hand on his green, warty shoulder. 'We can do it together.'

'Nuh-uh!' Jiggy said. 'We need to get started on your hair, Willow, lickety-spit. Those braids won't plait themselves.'

'Og go alone,' Ogden pouted.

'Here.' Fenella delved into the trunk, and brought out a vibrant pink boa, with tiny jewels nestled amongst the gold-tipped feathers. 'Something to keep you going until you get back.'

'Oooh!' Ogden beamed a happy smile as he wrapped the boa carefully around his neck. 'Thanks, Aunty. Og be right back.' He looked at Jiggy. 'Lickety-spits.' He picked up the basket of Ratifers and headed off.

Ogden carried the Ratifers all the way to the village, and down the cobbled road to the jailhouse. Once inside, he opened the heavy wooden door of the jail room, where there were now three jail cells with strong iron bars to keep the monsters in. All of the cells were full. Ogden sighed. Aunty Fenella was right. He really hadn't been clearing up his monsters. There was barely room for anyone else. He'd been spending so much time dancing, he was getting behind on his Guard Ogre duties. He set the wicker basket in the corner of the room, and opened the lid quickly to give the Ratifers a bowl of water and some chunks of bread to eat. He shut the lid firmly again. The ratties would be fine in their basket until tomorrow.

'Purrrr-la hissss!'

Ogden turned to look at the large, white furry creature that was locked in the cell furthest away from him. It had a pink nose with whiskers, big, green eyes, and a grumpy look on its feline face.

'Purr-fluffla hisss, purrla-flort!'

it said crossly.

'Yes, yes, Giant Catkins, Og fetch you foods too.' Ogden trundled over to the creature, gathering up a handful of fish biscuits from a sack and chucking them in

under the bars. The Catkins munched the biscuits hungrily.

'Fleeble-weeble, peep, peep, peep!'

A couple of angry-looking miniature dragons flapped indignantly from the middle cell.

'Foods for yous too.' Ogden poked some slices of bread through the bars. The dragons breathed fire on the bread and turned it into toast, which they crunched, loudly.

'Sleuuuuuuuuuurch.' A massive, oozy slug made a yucky-sucky sound from the last cell.

'Og knows you likes leaves.' Ogden opened a window, reached to the nearest tree, and snapped off a branch full of juicy, green

48

leaves. He poked it through the bars for the slug, who snacked on the leaves, slurpily.

'Now yous have full tummies, monsters. Be goods. For tomorrow Og will take yous far-far away, to place where yous be happy, and not bothering the villagers with your monstery ways.'

He carefully locked the door and left the jail, and was about to walk back to Willow's house, when he heard a stern voice behind him.

'Stop!'

Ogden turned to see a crowd of villagers gathered in the street. A very angry-looking man at the front of the group spoke.

'Ogre!' the angry man sneered. 'Call yourself a detective?'

Ogden thought some thoughts. 'Og call

Og Ogden.' He stuck out a huge, gnarly hand. 'Pleased to meets you.'

'No.' The man ignored Ogden's hand and growled at him. 'You and that little girl call yourselves the Monster Mashers, don't you?'

Ogden smiled. 'You are right, tall, angry man.'

'You hunt monsters wearing pink feathers round your neck, do you?' The man looked at Ogden's boa scornfully.

'Yes,' Ogden agreed. 'Or sometimes red ones.'

Angry Man looked even angrier. He reached forward and tugged at the boa, and it fell to the ground. Ogden's eyes widened, and he suppressed a furious snort, drawing himself up to his full height and glowering at the man.

'Let's all keep calm, shall we?' Someone pushed to the front of the crowd. It was Ogden's friend, the baker. He picked up the boa and shook the dust off it, handing it back. 'Now, Ogden, you know how much I like you. No one eats as many of my cakes as you do.'

Ogden nodded proudly. 'A cake a day keeps the tummy grumbles away.'

'Er, yes,' said the baker, patting Ogden on the back. 'But the thing is . . . our food is being scumfished by those Ratifers, and we're all a little worried that you and Willow are letting things slip.'

'Don't worries, Bakerman.' Ogden patted the baker on his back, almost knocking him over. 'Og put the Ratifers in the jail. No more nibbles for them.'

'That's good news, indeed.' The

baker's mouth formed a thin line. 'But unfortunately, that's not everything—'

'We won't hear a word against this ogre!' A voice came from the back of the crowd. Two more villagers came forward. It was the cobbler and his wife. They were carrying three squirmy toddlers.

'This ogre saved my babes when they were only wee!' the cobbler's wife said. 'Have you all forgotten?'

'That's right.' The Mayor hurried up to the crowd, his chunky, golden necklace bouncing on his chest. 'Don't you remember how he chased away the Spiny Minotaur? Caught the Dribbly Flibbertigibbet, and told the Whiz Wasps to buzz off? He and Willow are heroes.'

'Yes, but ever since disco fever hit the valley, the Monster Mashers have barely been around,' the grocer woman said. She looked up at Ogden. 'I'm glad you've caught the Ratifers. They were taking all my fruit and veg. But we have bigger problems now.'

'Much bigger!'
shouted Angry Man.

'What Danger-monsters lurk?' Ogden said. 'For I will catch 'em. Whatevers they steal, I will get it back again, Mayorman.'

'I hope so, Ogden.' The Mayor shook his head. 'Because food is not the only thing that has been disappearing around here.'

Ogden frowned at him. 'What yous mean?'

The Mayor looked very serious. 'People are disappearing too, Ogden. Our grannies are gone.'

'Gone?' Ogden said.

'Three so far – Granny Grunter, Granny Magee, and Granny Smith. We don't know what to do.' The Mayor looked at Ogden, shaking his head, sadly. 'Please say you can help us?'

Ogden ran back to the tree house as quickly as his legs would carry him. He tried to remember all that the Mayorman had told him. But he was oh-so sleepy from being up all night catching Ratifers, and things were getting mixed up in his head. He thought some thoughts. Had the Mayorman really said that grannies were going missing? But Jiggy was a granny, and she hadn't gone anywhere. It was all very confusing.

As he neared the clearing, he could hear the jumpety-bumpety noise coming from

Jiggy's boom box. Willow was practising the Boogaloo, her hair in tiny plaits, glittery beads clicking together as she danced. She spotted him, and turned the music off.

'Ogden! There you are, at last.' She went to grab his gnarly hand. 'Time's ticking. What have you been doing?'

Ogden opened his mouth to tell her, but before he could, Fenella grabbed his other hand and pulled him over to a tree stump.

'No time for yakkety-yakking now,' Fenella said, pushing him gently but firmly onto the stump. 'You need to get ready before we set off for the Big Disco Night.'

Ogden opened his mouth to speak again, but Jiggy jumped in before he could say anything.

'And I still haven't taught you the Mashed Potato, Ogden,' Jiggy said, frowning.

Ogden's tummy rumbled. He hadn't eaten anything all day. 'Scrumptious,' he murmured. 'Og very hungry for mash tatoes.'

Willow laughed. 'No, Ogden! The Mashed Potato is another disco dance. Jiggy? **Music, please!**'

Jiggy hit a button on the boom box and the jumpety-bumpety music started again. Ogden watched as Willow started to wiggle her hips, making fists with her hands and putting them one on top of the other in time to the music. She grinned at him. 'Like this!'

Ogden copied her from his seat on the tree trunk, as Fenella held up the sparkliest, twirly-whirliest dress he'd ever seen.

'Rainbow colours, Ogden!' she said. 'What do you think?'

'Ogden love it,' he said, reaching out to touch the shimmering fabric. Dresses were his favourite. The rainbow sparkles made his heart sing, and he loved to feel the skirt fly out as he danced. With all his dancing finery on, he never felt like a big, lumbering ogre. He was as light as a feather, a glittering jewel, a beautiful, proud peacock.

Fenella slipped the dress over his huge head, and began to pull a pair of shiny, pink platform boots onto his two left feet.

As Ogden gazed down at all the sparkling sequins, Fenella plonked a frizzy, fuchsia wig on his head. 'A perfect fit!' she said, grabbing her make-up brush. 'Now, just a touch of glam on your face, and you're done, you betcha!' She dabbed at his cheeks and glitter blew everywhere. Ogden watched the tiny pieces twinkle in the air, and thought hard. Now, what was it he had to tell them again?

'Stop!' He held up a warty hand. 'Stop everything!'

Willow stopped dancing, and Fenella looked at him in surprise. Jiggy pressed a button and the music came to a halt. Ogden took a breath. 'Og has important news to tells.'

'Yes?' Willow looked at him, concerned.

'Something's wrong?' said Fenella.

Ogden nodded, slowly.

'Spit it out, dude,' said Jiggy.

Ogden took another breath, his wig wobbling on his head.

'Granny,' he said, firmly. 'Gone.'

'What?' said Willow. 'Jiggy's here, Ogden.' She looked at the others, and grabbed Ogden's hand. 'Poor Ogden, he's tired and hungry. Here –' she sat him down on a nearby picnic blanket and handed him a slice of something delicious-looking – 'I saved you some Spin-much Pie, it's your favourite.'

Ogden swallowed the pie in one swallow, and shook his head. 'No, Little Wills. Not Granny Jiggy, but other ones . . .' He crinkled his brow. 'Mayorman says the grannies, theys disappear.'

Willow frowned, and gave him a shiny apple. 'Well, Ogden . . . sometimes, when grannies get very, very old—'

'No, like the foods the Ratifers stole,' Ogden said, rubbing his eyes. 'Mayorman said Granny Smiths is missing.'

'Oh!' Fenella said. 'You mean apples?' She pointed to the fruit in his hand. 'A Granny Smith is a type of apple, Ogden. That's what they must have meant.'

'Yes!' said Willow. 'The Ratifers were eating all the villagers' fruit and veg. Climbing the trees in the orchard and stealing the apples!'

'But you caught the Ratifers, Ogden.' Jiggy patted him on his sequined back. 'No more food will go missing – no more "grannies" will disappear. Job done! Now on your feet, disco dancer – there's work to do.'

She turned on the boom box and music filled the air. Ogden shrugged and stood up, the music wiggling its way into his body and making him want to dance.

'To the disco!' Willow led the way across the clearing to the path to the village. They danced all the way, carrying Jiggy's boom box and her glitter ball, only slowing down when they arrived in the empty cobbled street in front of the village hall. Fenella turned the music off.

'Jeepers Creepers, where did everyone go?' Jiggy said.

'We must be late. Everyone is inside already,' Willow said.

'So quietly-quiet,' Ogden said, trotting along after Willow on his platform boots.

'There'll be loud jumpety-bumpety music, just you wait,' Willow said, reaching the village hall. 'Bright lights flashing, everyone laughing, dressed to the nines, grooving to the funky beat!' She grabbed the handle of the door to the hall, and flung it open. 'Ta-da!'

But there was no jumpety-bumpety music. No flashing lights. And no one was laughing.

Ogden, Willow, Fenella and Jiggy stepped inside and looked around. Everyone was glumly sitting at the side of the dance floor. No one was wearing sparkly disco clothes. The golden disco trophy was on its

own on a table at the far end of the hall.

'What's happened to the disco?' said Willow, to the villagers. 'We brought our glitter ball.' She held it up. 'Why is no one dancing?'

The Mayor got up from the nearest bench and walked towards the friends.

'The disco has been cancelled,' he said, looking at their clothes. 'Didn't Ogden tell you the news?'

'Of course he didn't!' A man stood up at the back. Ogden recognised him as the tall, angry man he'd met earlier in the day.

Angry Man walked up to him and snarled, 'We told you what had happened, ogre, but you don't care. Too busy getting into your disco clothes to do anything about it, eh?'

'What are you talking about?' Willow said, putting her hands on her hips and puffing out her chest. 'What could be so important?'

'Grannies are going missing, that's what,' the Mayor called out. 'You should be out there looking for them, and catching whoever has taken them.' He sighed and crossed his arms. 'Ogden, I thought better of you.'

'Wait a moment, what's this?' Willow said. 'Ogden did try to tell us something, but we didn't understand him. He said Granny Smiths had gone missing. We thought he was talking about apples!'

'Certainly not,' said the Mayor, crossly.

'Well, what are we waiting for?' Willow said. 'Never fear, the Monster Mashers are here!' She stomped up to the door and flung it open. 'Come on, Ogden! Let's find these grannies, and then we'll be back to win that trophy, you'll see!'

Willow strutted out of the village hall, followed by Ogden, Fenella and Jiggy, and the villagers trooped out onto the cobbled street behind them. The sun had almost set, and the warm, orange glow of the oil street lamps was the only light to be seen.

'I'm sorry I didn't understand what you meant,' Willow whispered to Ogden. 'I really wasn't using my good listening ears.'

Ogden gently tugged at one of Willow's earlobes. 'That's OK, Little Will. Hard to listen when ears full of jumpety-bumpety music.'

'Very true.' Willow gave him a wink. 'This way!' She started down the road. 'We're off to find those grannies!'

Fenella stopped in her tracks. 'Wait a minute, Willow. Where exactly are we going?'

'Oh! Er, yes,' Willow said. 'Well, what do detectives do? We review the evidence.' She turned to the Mayor. 'Tell us everything you know.'

The Mayor nodded. 'The first granny to go missing was Granny Grunter,' he said, panting a little. 'You know, the lovely lady who has the knitting shop, here in the village?'

'Yup,' said Ogden. 'Og tried to eat her once. She poked Og in the tum with a knitting needle.'

'Whoa,' said Jiggy. 'That's not cool, Ogden.'

'No, she was not cool,' agreed Ogden. 'She was hot from trying to runs away from big, scary ogre.'

'But that was before you gave up eating people, wasn't it, Ogden?' said Willow, hurriedly. 'He's on a very strict diet, these days, everybody.'

'Never mind about that,' said the Mayor. 'Back to the problem in hand. Granny Grunter was last seen sitting on the park bench, by the babbling brook. We searched for her, but all we found was a big ball of wool.'

'Hmm, curious,' said Willow. 'She was last seen on the park bench? Then that's where we start looking! Follow me!' She

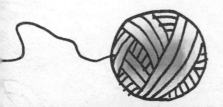

set off along the cobbled road, towards the woods.

'But wait!' The Mayor said. 'Then there was Granny Magee,' he said. 'She was reading *The Daily Bagpipe* newspaper under the big oak tree in the meadow. There was no sign of her, except for a knitting pattern, and her horn-rimmed glasses.'

'Hmm. Them glasses not tasty, that's why the monster did not eats them,' considered Ogden. 'Scratchy in the throats.' He rubbed his neck.

'The grannies have been eaten?' Angry Man shouted, and the villagers began to moan and cry.

'No, no!' said Willow. 'We don't know these grannies were eaten! They're just missing.'

She whispered to Ogden out of the corner of her mouth. 'Let's think positive, detective.'

She turned to the crowd. 'To the meadow!' She turned round and started to walk up the hill to the meadow.

'But there's more!' the Mayor interrupted. 'Don't forget Granny Smith. She was having a little rest on the stone wall by the drinking well.' He sniffed, sadly. 'All we found was her knitting needles, and a bag of boiled sweets.'

'Terribly-terrible!' said Ogden, appalled. 'Why would a Danger-monster leave the yummy sweeties?'

'Ogden!' Willow hissed at him. 'That's not the point.' She frowned. 'Right. The drinking well. Let's start there, then.' She turned to go down the hill again.

'So this is what you do?' said Jiggy.

'And I thought the Monster Mash was a dance!'

'I'm not sure this is a good idea,' Fenella called to Willow. 'It's getting dark, you betcha.'

'**Help! Help!**' A voice cried from somewhere down the street. 'Come quickly!'

Willow and Ogden looked at each other, turned, and set off sprinting, their disco clothes glinting in the street lamps as they ran. The villagers followed.

A boy was standing on the bridge, waving his hands in the air.

'Quickly! Over here!'

Willow and Ogden reached him first. He pointed to the babbling brook below the bridge.

'Something came out from under the bridge and grabbed my granny!' he panted.

Ogden leaped over the side of the bridge down to the riverbank below. It was very dark. He searched, stomping along the riverbank in his platform boots, but there was nothing to be seen apart from the shallow water. He scratched his head underneath his huge, pink wig. What monster could have been so fast?

Meanwhile, up on the bridge, the Mayor and everyone else had arrived at the scene. Ogden climbed up to see them.

'Freddo Fuzzbun!' the Mayor said, throwing his arms around the boy. 'You're safe now.'

'But my granny!' bawled Freddo.

'We'll find her!' Willow said.

'Nothing downs there,' Ogden said.

'Tell us what happened, Freddo,' said Willow.

The boy took a breath. 'We were on our way to the village hall, when Granny dropped her lucky thimble into the stream,' said Freddo. 'We were standing on the bridge, looking for it, when something big and scary flew up and got her!'

'Big and scary? What did the monster look like?' said Willow. 'Did it say anything? Which way did it go?' She questioned the boy urgently. But all Freddo could do was sob.

'There, there,' Fenella said. 'I'm your neighbour, we know each other, don't we, Freddo?' The boy nodded. 'Don't you worry about your granny, the Monster Mashers are here to help you.'

'Everyone should go home, where it's safe,' the Mayor said. 'Fenella and I will take Freddo home to his mum and dad,

and the Monster Mashers will
do their detective work.'

'Take this lantern, Willow,'
Fenella said, handing her the light.
'And be careful! Are you coming
with me, Jiggy?'

'No way, girl,' Jiggy said. 'If I'm not going
to disco tonight, I'm monster mashing!'

Everyone left, apart from Ogden,
Willow and Jiggy, who made their way
down to the riverbank again.

'We have to search for clues,' Willow
said. 'Footprints, trampled grass –
anything that might tell us which way the
monster took Granny Fuzzbun.'

'Maybe it will come back,' said Jiggy.
She looked into the water. 'Hmm.
If you want to catch a fish, you need to use
some bait . . .'

'Stay close, Little Will and Jiggy,' said Ogden. 'Sometime the Danger-monsters lurk in the shadow.'

'Good to know,' Jiggy shivered.

'This Granny Gobbler is a tricksy one,' said Ogden. 'And fast too.'

'Granny Gobbler?' said Jiggy. 'You seem very sure about that, Ogden. Maybe we should come back in the morning?'

'Let's search for a few more minutes.' Willow pressed ahead. 'There are lives at stake!'

They walked on, until they reached a fork in the stream.

'I'll check this way with Jiggy. Ogden, you go that way,' Willow said, heading down the left branch of the stream. 'Anything?'

'Big fat zero!' said Jiggy.

'No grannies, no gobblers.' Ogden shrugged his hairy shoulders.

'Wait!' Willow said, shining her lantern on the water. 'See there, on the rock in the brook? A giant feather! It's closer to you, Og. Can you reach it?'

'Wheres?' Ogden replied. 'Can'ts see.'

'I'll come round with the light!' Willow raced back to the fork in the stream, and crossed over to Ogden. 'It's just there!' She pointed the lantern, and Ogden carefully put a platform-booted foot on a stepping stone.

'Er, Willowtree?' Jiggy called from the darkness. 'Can you hear something coming?'

'No. What?' said Willow, still watching Ogden reaching for the feather.

'Not so much a sound, but a beat. A beat, through my feet.' Jiggy lowered her hands to the soft grass. 'Can you feel it too?'

Willow shook her head, impatiently. 'This is no time for disco, Granny.'

'Ooh!' Jiggy said, excitedly. 'Hold the front page! Here's the lucky thimble, lying in the grass!' She held it up, waving it in the air at Willow and Ogden.

Thud!
Thud! Thud!

'Gobble,
gobble,
gobble!'

Suddenly a giant bird came running out of the darkness towards Jiggy.

'Holy moly, Chicken Licken!' cried Jiggy.

'It's . . . a turkey,' Willow gasped.

The bird was immense, almost the size of two Ogdens put together. His body was covered in black feathers, with huge, scratchy claws on the end of his scaly legs. As he reached Jiggy, he fanned out his tail feathers, raised his head and blinked at her with his one big, gloopy eye.

'A Lurkey-Turkey!' said Ogden.

'Gobble, gobble, gobble!' The bird shook his long, fleshy wattle, opened his enormous beak and plucked Jiggy off the ground by the seat of her satin disco pants.

'Put that granny down!' yelled Willow, splashing through the stream towards them,

Ogden hot on her heels. But they couldn't reach the Lurkey-Turkey in time.

'Whaaaaa!' Jiggy yelled, as the bird flipped her over his head. She landed on his back neatly, and clung to his feathers for dear life, as he spun round. 'Ogden! Willowtree!' she shouted. 'Help meeeeeeeee!'

With that, the Lurkey-Turkey took off into the air with Jiggy, leaving Ogden and Willow standing, dripping and helpless, on the ground below.

Ogden and Willow could do nothing but watch as the huge bird took off into the darkening skies, with poor Jiggy clinging to its back.

'Graaaaaaaanny!' Willow yelled. 'Don't panic, we'll find you!' She turned to Ogden. 'They're flying over the village, towards the woods, I think. We have to follow, quickly!'

Ogden stretched up on his tippy-toes to get a better look, but the turkey was out of sight.

'Come on!' Willow grabbed his hands, and the two of them scrambled up the riverbank, and started to run. Willow's lantern cast a little light on the path, but when they reached the trees, the flame started to flicker as if it was going to go out. 'We have to find them, Ogden,' Willow said, urgently. 'Now, think. Where would a monster like that live? Where would it hide?'

Og shook his head. 'Them Lurkey-Turkeys likes to nest up trees. Big, big trees. But this is the woods . . . oh-so-many trees to search.'

Willow sat down on a stump, and a big, fat tear rolled down her cheek.

'This is hopeless, Ogden!' she cried. 'I'm so frightened for Jiggy! What will that terrible turkey do to her?'

Ogden knelt down beside her, and patted her head gently. 'Don't worries, Little

Will. Them turkeys don't eats people, they eats cranberries, of course.' He nodded confidently.

But Willow only sobbed more and more loudly. 'Then what does it want Jiggy for?' she howled. 'And all of the other grannies? Why is it taking them away?'

Ogden thought some thoughts, really, really hard, trying his hardest to find an answer to Willow's question. But the answer wasn't there. Instead, he hugged Willow, then stood up straight. He put on his firmest Willow-voice.

'Stand ups, dancer! Yous never gives up, do yous, detective?'

Willow looked up at him, and burst out laughing, in spite of her tears. 'You're right, Og. It's no use sitting here, crying. We need to use our brains!'

Ogden pulled Willow up. She looked at him in the flickering lamplight, with a brave smile on her face.

'I've got a plan, Ogden. But we're going to need Aunty Fenella to help us.'

Ogden smiled back at her. 'You betcha!'

The streets were completely empty when Ogden and Willow arrived back at the village. As they arrived at Fenella's Fashions, Willow shivered. 'It's so quiet. Perhaps everyone is hiding from the Lurkey-Turkey?'

'But Lurkey-Turkey only takes grannies.' Ogden frowned.

'That's what I'm counting on,' said Willow, as she knocked on the door of the shop. The door opened slowly, and Aunty Fenella peered out.

'There you are!' Fenella said. 'I was so worried!' She let them in, shutting the door behind them all, quickly. Fenella's shop was a mess of material, feathers, sequins and thread, with a worktable at one end, and a fireman's pole in the middle of the room. 'Wait a minute – where's Jiggy?'

'Now, Aunty,' said Willow. 'There's good news, and bad news.' She tried to smile. 'The good news is, we've found the monster who's taken all the grannies. It's a Lurkey-Turkey, and Ogden says that it's OK, Lurkey-Turkeys don't eat people, so the grannies are probably all completely safe. That is good news, isn't it?'

'A Lurkey-Turkey?' said Fenella, grimly. 'I've heard stories about them, but I never thought they were real.'

She raised an eyebrow. 'And what's the bad news?'

'Bad news is, Lurkey-Turkey nabbed Jiggy,' Ogden said.

'What?!' Fenella said. 'It took Mama?'

'Yup,' said Ogden.

'No!' Fenella groaned. 'That's terrible!'

'Yes, terribly-terrible,' agreed Ogden. 'The naughty turkey flews off with her on his back.' He flapped his arms like wings. 'Uh-oh! And we don't knows where he gone.'

'Oh!' Fenella's eyes rolled up into her head, and she collapsed into a chair, moaning.

Willow fanned her with a sewing pattern. 'Don't worry, I've got a plan!' she said. 'And you need to be strong, Aunty, because I'm going to need all the help you can give me.' Fenella sat up a little, and Willow ran around the shop, picking up odd pieces of material and holding them against her. 'We'll need to work quickly to make me a costume.'

'What?' said Fenella.

'No time for disco now, Little Will,' Ogden said.

'No,' Willow agreed. 'But Jiggy gave me an idea, when she said that to catch the monster, we would need some bait. What does the Lurkey-Turkey like? Grannies. So I'll be the bait. I'll dress up as a granny, he will come to us, and we'll catch him.'

'Hold your horses,' said Fenella. 'It's very risky.'

'I'll be fine,' Willow said, firmly. 'I've been thinking about it. What do the grannies have in common? They were all nabbed by the babbling brook – in the meadow, by the oak tree, the wishing well and the bridge. And that makes sense, because the Lurkey-Turkey eats the cranberries that grow in the water. So I'll dress up as a granny and wait by the brook.' Willow tried on a floppy hat. 'Does this look grannyish enough?'

'I won't allow it!' Fenella said.

'Lurkey-Turkey might nab yous too, Little Will,' said Ogden, seriously.

'Not if you catch him in your net, Ogden,' Willow said. 'It's the best plan, admit it!'

Fenella thought a little, and eventually she nodded. 'I can run something up by morning. Ogden can go to the jailhouse, get his net, and then he can help me finish the costume. You –' she pointed at Willow – 'get to bed.' Willow started to protest, but Fenella shook her head. 'You're going to need your rest.'

Willow did as she was told. She climbed the stairs, took off her disco clothes and crept into Fenella's comfy, purple bed. As she lay there, she thought some thoughts. Why had the grannies been taken? It still didn't make sense. Willow tossed and turned. But finally, in spite of the worries dancing around her head, the sound of Fenella's sewing machine soon lulled her into a deep, deep sleep.

When Willow awoke in the morning, she dressed in her dungarees and running shoes that had magically appeared at the end of the bed. She slid down the fireman's pole into the shop below, to find Fenella and Ogden waiting for her.

'We're finished!' Fenella cried. She gathered up a huge pile of spotty, pink satin, and held it up. 'Very chic, you betcha!' Attached to the dress there was an apron with pink sequins on, and Fenella also held a mob cap with pink feathers sewn around the bottom of it. She grinned. 'The perfect costume for the perfect granny.'

'But Aunty, that's way too big for me!' Willow said. 'And it doesn't look right. Grannies don't dress up in sparkles.'

'Granny Jiggy does,' said Ogden.

'Well, she does,' admitted Willow. 'But normal grannies don't look like that.'

'Who wants to be normal?' said Fenella, shrugging.

'I don'ts!' Ogden shouted, putting his hand in the air.

'We know that,' Fenella said. She winked at Willow. 'I didn't make this costume for you, Willow. This costume is for Ogden.'

'Sparkly granny!' Ogden beamed.

'But . . .' Willow blinked.

'This turkey won't know what's hit him.' Fenella threw the dress over Ogden's head. 'Glam Granny Ogden will show him who's boss, you betcha!'

Granny Ogden stepped out into the street, his pink satin dress shining in the morning sun. His cheeks were red, his lips painted the same colour as his dress, and he was wearing a pale blue curly wig underneath his sparkly mob cap. He was the most gorgeous granny in the land.

'This is so heavy,' Willow panted, as she and Fenella dragged a large washing basket out of the door after him. 'What's in it, Aunty?'

'Something to help us catch the Granny Gobbler,' whispered Fenella, as she shut the door behind them. 'A net, to throw over the beast. And I've covered it up in the basket with clothes: jumpers, scarves, hats – and some of my dirty undies – for Ogden to pretend to wash in the brook.'

'Urgh!' said Willow. 'Dirty undies?'

'They're not really dirty,' said Fenella. 'It's just pretend, isn't it, Og?'

'You betcha, Aunty.' Og winked at her, his fluttering eyelashes painted blue to match his hair. 'Og not only a dancer, Og can do pretend too,' he said, proudly, picking up the washing basket easily.

'I hope so,' said Willow. 'Now, let's find a quiet spot by the brook where nobody else will be around.'

They quickly and quietly made their way through the village and disappeared into the woods, following the path until they reached the babbling brook.

'Where should we start?' Fenella said.

Willow looked around. 'There's a big cranberry bog over there. We'll hide in that bush beside it, and Ogden, you start washing your woollies and undies in the water.'

Ogden giggled.

'This is serious, Og!' Willow said. 'We must keep on our toes. The Lurkey-Turkey could be anywhere.'

Everyone looked from right to left and all around, nervously.

'Positions, everyone!' Willow said. She beckoned to Fenella and the two of them disappeared behind a bush.

Ogden cleared his throat, straightened

his apron and, with a deep breath, carried his basket of washing over to the sparkling waters of the brook. With a quick glance from side to side, he bent low, picked up a large, woolly jumper, and started to wash it . . . and sing.

'Oh, a washer-granny, that's what I is!
I wash all day, like this, and this!
Nobody but Granny,
For miles and miles,
I wash and wash
And smile my smiles!'

'What on earth is he doing?' Fenella muttered.

'Sssh!' said Willow, furiously. 'He's . . . pretending.'

The two watched as Ogden washed and hummed, all the time sneaking little glances up and down the riverbank. He had nearly finished all the washing, when Willow heard something . . . or rather, felt something.

Thud!

Willow's eyes widened. She grabbed Fenella's arm. 'It's coming!'

Thud! Thud! Thud! Thud!

'Whatever it is, it's big!' Willow could feel the beat of the earth below her. 'We'd

better warn Ogden.'

'Too late for that.' Fenella was pointing though the bushes.

As they looked towards the brook, they saw the huge, one-eyed bird strutting towards Ogden. He looked even scarier in the daylight. The Lurkey-Turkey was black as ink, with dirty white tips on his feathers. His long wattle of crinkly neck-skin wobbled ferociously as he walked. His feet were red and scaly, and his beak was bright yellow and sharp-looking.

He stopped, just short of Ogden's turned back, and made a low sound.

'Gobble, gobble, gobble!'

'Woollies and pullies
and scarfs and socks
Put 'em in the water and
scrub 'em on the rocks!'

Ogden sang on, not hearing the Lurkey-Turkey.

'Rub 'em and rinse 'em,
      my clothes so clean!
Best washer-granny you ever seen!'

'Oh my goodness, we have to warn him,' gasped Willow. But it was too late.

The giant turkey pulled itself up to its full height, fanned out its tail and raised its sharp beak into the air. 'Gobble, gobble!'

This time, Ogden heard. He stood up.

'Ogden!' Willow cried, running out from behind the bushes. Ogden turned, and as he did, the turkey ran at him with all its might, knocking him over into the brook with a splash. He sat up in the water, shaking the drops from his blue wig, and looking around him in surprise.

The Lurkey-Turkey was too quick for him. It jumped upon him with its massive claws, pushing him down into the babbling brook.

'No!' Willow shouted. Fenella grabbed her before she could run to him.

The Lurkey-Turkey startled, and Ogden pushed him off, spluttering out of the water. His big dress was soaked and dragging him down. His mob cap and blue wig were sliding down the back of his head, and his make-up was half-washed off in the water. The Lurkey-Turkey flapped its wings and dashed at Ogden, flat out.

'Watch out!' Willow cried.

Ogden bounded up from the brook,

grabbing at the net in his washing basket. But he wasn't quick enough. The Lurkey-Turkey bashed into him, and the basket flew into the air, net and undies and all. The furious turkey grabbed Ogden's arm with one claw, and stunned him on the head with a peck. Ogden fell onto the soft ground with a thud.

'Og!' Willow broke free from Fenella, but it was too late. Odgen's eyes were tight closed, and he looked as if nothing would wake him up now.

The giant bird grabbed Ogden's dress with one of its big, pink claws, and threw him onto his back. The turkey gave a final 'gobble, gobble, gobble!' and galloped off into the woods, Ogden slumped and bouncing around on top, his shiny dress flowing out behind him. The turkey kept trying to flap its wings and take off, but Ogden was too heavy for him to carry up into the air.

'After them!' shouted Willow, and she ran as fast as her legs would go, Fenella close on her heels. 'We won't lose them this time!' In the distance, they could only just see the Lurkey-Turkey fleeing through the trees, as Ogden was carried further and further into the woods.

The chase was on!

'Ogden! Wake up! The Lurkey-Turkey has got you!' Willow shouted, as she and Fenella ran as fast as they could, dodging past trees, jumping over logs and clumps of grass, and leaping over streams and patches of stinging nettles. They ran until Willow thought her heart would jump out of her chest, and her toes would drop off. Just as she thought she would have to stop, the turkey slowed down at the bottom of the widest, tallest, knobbliest oak tree Willow had ever seen.

'Wake up, Ogden!' Willow panted

again, but she was so puffed she could barely get the words out. She leaned on a tree and tried to get her breath back.

Still unable to fly, the Lurkey-Turkey turned round and snagged the collar of Ogden's dress in his beak. The giant bird started to climb the gnarly oak, hauling up the sleeping Ogden.

Fenella caught up with Willow, and collapsed on a grassy hillock. 'What is it doing? What's up there?'

Willow crept forward, carefully, and looked into the thick branches of the great oak. The Lurkey-Turkey climbed high, before it plonked a sleeping Ogden onto a large, flat branch.

'Ogden!' Willow called. 'Wake up!'

'Be careful, Willow!' Fenella whispered.

'It's OK, Aunty,' Willow replied. 'The

turkey's climbing higher.' She peered up the tree, shading her eyes from the sun with her hand. 'Ooh! He's got a nest. He's sitting on it.' **Plop!**

Something soft and round hit Willow on the head. **Plop! Plop!**

Two more hits.

Plop! Plop! Plop!

Willow bent down to pick up one of the things that had hit her. It was a fuzzy ball of soft, pink wool.

'The Lurkey-Turkey's throwing wool at me?' she puzzled. 'How strange!'

'Cooooo-eeee!'

A voice came from high up in the tree.

'Ogden?' Willow peered up into the branches again, but Ogden was still slumbering.

'I'm not Ogden! Don't you recognise

your own grandmother?'

Willow looked further along the branch where Ogden was sleeping. She saw someone waving.

'Jiggy!' she cried. 'Are you OK?'

'This is far out, Willowtree!' Jiggy cried. 'I've never been so high. I can see all the way to the Purple Mountains!'

'But are you hurt?' Fenella called. 'Did the turkey do you any harm?'

'No way,' Jiggy said. 'We're cool. But I think my friends would like a cup of elderberry tea.'

'We?' Willow said. 'Your friends?'

Voices came from behind the green leaves.

'Hello there!'

'Pleased to meet you!'

'Ooh, have you brought tea?'

'And a lovely biscuit?'

Willow looked even further along the branch. Four grannies were sitting there, chuckling to themselves.

'Granny Grunter? Granny Magee?' Willow called. 'Granny Smith and Granny Fuzzbun?'

One by one, the grannies called out.

'Here!'

'Present and correct!'

'Have you come to get us down?

'And you've brought a lovely biscuit?'

'Oh my goodness!' Willow ran to the base of the tree, and started to climb.

'Yes, we will get you down, don't worry!' She pulled herself up the tree. There were lots of easy low branches and footholds.

'Careful, Willow,' Fenella said from below. 'What if you slip and fall? And what if the turkey comes down from his nest again?'

'Pah, I won't fall!' Willow said, climbing higher still. 'And if we're quick – and quiet,' she hissed, 'we'll all get down before he even notices.'

She climbed all the way up until she was just below the branch where Ogden, Jiggy and all the grannies were.

'Pssst, Ogden!' she said. 'Time to wake up now! You need to help me rescue these grannies.'

'**Snooooorrrrre!**' Ogden snoozed on, his shiny dress fluttering in the breeze.

'Wakey-wakey!' Willow tried again. But it was no use, he wouldn't wake up.

'Right.' Willow looked down at Fenella on the ground. 'Throw up some of those balls of wool, will you, Aunty?' Fenella frowned at her, but did as she was asked, tossing three balls up to Willow, who caught them deftly, with one hand. Tucking two balls under her arm, she shut one eye, took aim, and hurled the first ball at Ogden.

Bop!

It bonked on his head.

But Ogden slept on.

Sock!

The second ball thumped him in the tummy.

But still he snored.

Thock!

The third clonked him on the nose.

But he didn't wake up.

'Oh, Ogden!' Willow hissed at him. 'You're impossible!'

'How's it hanging, Willowtree?' called Jiggy, from along the branch.

'Not very well,' said Willow. 'Ogden won't wake up. Is there any way you can climb down on your own?'

'Hmm, not sure about that,' Jiggy said. 'Not wearing these platform boots, anyhow.' She pulled them off, one by one, and threw them to the ground with a bump. 'Hmm,' she wiggled her toes.

'I might be the granny with the groove, but my tree-climbing days were way back in the day. Any different ideas?'

'I'm working on it,' Willow said. 'What about the rest of you ladies, can you climb down?'

'My bottom is sore!'

'I'm not as nimble as I used to be!'

'Are you bringing a ladder?'

'And a lovely biscuit?'

'You can't carry us, Willowtree,' shrugged Jiggy. 'Looks like we're hanging tight. Unless you can get a ladder.'

Willow shook her head. 'Even the longest ladder in the land wouldn't reach this high.'

Jiggy sighed. 'Then without Ogden's help, what do we do, little Boo? We need to get on down, and for once, I don't mean disco.'

Willow thought for a minute. 'Disco! That's it, Jiggy! We need to wake Ogden up, and what is the best way to do that? Play him some jumpety-bumpety music. I've got to get your boom box!'

Willow climbed down the tree as fast as she could safely go. Fenella was waiting for her at the bottom.

'I heard what you said about the boom box,' Fenella said. 'While you were asleep last night, Ogden took the boom box and the glitter ball back to the tree house when he collected your clothes.'

'I'll be faster on my own, Aunty,' Willow said. 'Stay here, but stay out of sight of the Lurkey-Turkey. Keep an eye on the grannies, I'll be back before you can

115

say Funky Chicken. And before I go,' she said, reaching down to pick something off the ground, 'I'd better collect some of those balls of wool. I have a feeling I'm going to need them.'

Willow unravelled some wool from the first ball. It was red. She tied it around the trunk of the nearest oak tree, and set off running, trailing a strand of wool as she went. She and Fenella had run so fast they'd barely noticed which way they'd come, or how far they'd travelled. Without the wool, it would be impossible to find her way back to the Lurkey-Turkey's tree.

But which was the way to her tree house?

'Oh, sometimes I wish the woods had signposts!' she muttered to herself.

'Wouldn't that be easier?' Then she remembered a trick that Ogden had taught her on one of their monster-hunting expeditions. She looked upwards. Where was the sun? It was important not to look straight at it and get blinky-blinky sore eyes, but she just had to see how high it was in the sky. 'I know it's morning, and the sun is over there, in the east,' she said to herself. 'My tree house is east of the woods. So, if I run towards the sun, I should reach home.'

Off she went, running as fast as she could, unravelling the wool until she'd reached the end of the first ball. She quickly tied it to the second ball, a blue one. Then came an orange ball, and when she came to the end of that, she tied it to a purple one.

'I really hope I don't have to go much

further, I've only got one ball left!' She looked down at the green wool in her hand. Seeing the colour reminded her of Ogden, asleep on the tree. She had to hurry, she had to wake him up!

As she was halfway through the green ball of wool, the woods around her began to look more familiar, and then she recognised the way to the clearing where the tree house was. She tied the wool to a tree, and sprinted the rest of the way. She had made it!

Willow bounded up the ladder, onto the deck of the tree house.

'There!' She found the boom box and the glitter ball where Ogden had left them by her hammock. The boom box was quite heavy to carry down the ladder, but she managed it, puffing and panting. The big glitter ball was light as air, but awkward to carry. Luckily it had a circle of ribbon at the top, which she looped over her arm.

'Now, to follow the wool back!' She found the end of the green wool, and chased it until it became purple, orange, blue and finally, red. Just as she was winding the last of the wool back into a giant, multi-coloured ball, she heard noise coming through the trees.

'Chop the tree down!'

'No, burn it! That will be quicker!'

Then she heard Fenella's voice.

'Stop, this is madness!'

Willow arrived at the foot of the tree to see a group of villagers, led by Angry Man. He was carrying a large net, and some held axes or flaming torches. Their faces were flushed and furious.

'What's going on?'
Willow asked Fenella. 'Why are all the villagers shouting? Do they want the Lurkey-Turkey to notice and fly down here before we can get everyone away and safe?'

'Too late for that!' Fenella pointed up the tree. The Lurkey-Turkey was standing on top of his nest, his tail fanned out behind him.

'Gobble, gobble, gobble!'

Angry Man came up to Willow and Fenella. 'Stand aside, ladies. We will burn the tree down, and finish this once and for all!'

'Burn the tree . . . ?' Willow gasped. 'But the grannies are up there!'

Angry Man scowled at her. 'We have a net. They can jump down, and we'll save them.' He waved his flaming torch.

'And then we'll light the tree!'

'I'm not jumping!' said a voice, from far up in the branches.

'Ooh, that silly net doesn't look very safe!'

'You'll have to do better than that, young man!'

'And you'll have to bring biscuits!'

Willow grabbed hold of the man's torch. 'The grannies don't want to jump. And besides, my granny, Jiggy, is up there too, and Ogden.'

'Bah!' said Angry Man. 'As if we care about Ogden!'

'Well, I care about Ogden,' said Willow. 'And you should too. After everything he's done for us.' She set the boom box down on a tree stump. 'He'll save the day, just you wait and see!' She pressed a button.

Booga-wooga-wooga-woo!
Booga-wooga-wooga-woo!

The jumpety-bumpety disco music blared out into the woods.

'What's this?' snarled Angry Man.

'This is how we do things around here,' said Willow. She twirled the glitter ball around in the air. The tiny mirrors caught the sunlight and little rainbows of light danced through the forest. 'Watch.'

She pointed to Ogden. Sure enough, he began to move. His toes started to twitch, his shoulders to shake, and his head to roll from side to side.

'Funkadelic!' shouted Jiggy. 'Hold onto your hats, people!'

Ogden sat up on the branch. He looked at Jiggy. He looked down at Willow. And then he looked up at the Lurkey-Turkey.

'Og, you need to get the grannies down!'
shouted Willow, over the music.

Ogden didn't need telling twice.
He grabbed Jiggy under one strong arm,
and lifted her over his shoulder.

'Wheeee!' she cried.

He shimmied along the branch in time
to the disco beat, and gently held out his
hand for the first granny.

'Ooh, don't mind if I do, young man,'
said Granny Grunter, taking his hand.

He gently bundled her
under his arm and
jumped, deftly,
from branch to
branch until
he was on
the ground.

'Gobble, gobble!'
The Lurkey-Turkey was flapping his wings, and coming down the tree to the branch with the three remaining grannies on it.

'Ogden, quickly!' Willow cried.

He climbed the tree again, and was just in time to scoop up the remaining grannies. With Granny Magee on his back, and Granny Smith and Granny Fuzzbun under each arm, he leaped down the tree in time to the music, balancing expertly, with an ooooooooh and an eeeeeeeeeh from the villagers below.

'Keep thems safe!' He handed the grannies to the villagers, who helped them out of the way.

He looked up the tree. The turkey was nearly all the way down.

'Og, the net!' Willow pointed to where it was lying, on the ground beside the tree trunk. Ogden grabbed it, and was about to fling it up over the Lurkey-Turkey, when he tripped over a pile of some of the unravelled wool, and fell to the ground with a thump-bump-bump!

The turkey loomed over Ogden, his one eye glaring, his shiny, hooked beak dripping with turkey dribble.

'Ogden, no!' Willow called. Desperately she scrabbled around on the ground, and her hand found something smooth and shiny. It was one of Jiggy's golden platform boots. As the Lurkey-Turkey was about to pounce on her friend, Willow hurled the boot with all her might.

Thwack!

The boot hit the turkey on his big, feathery bottom. He turned round and gobbled furiously at Willow. She scrabbled in the grass again, found the second boot, and held it high, ready to throw.

'You better gobble off somewhere else, Lurkey-Turkey, or this boot is coming for you!' she cried. 'Leave our grannies alone and get out of our woods!' She held the boot a little higher, and glared at him ferociously. 'Or Ogden and I will lock you up in jail with the rest of the monsters!'

The turkey scratched the ground, as if he was going to charge. But behind him, Ogden had recovered and grabbed the net. To the side, the villagers were shouting too. The Lurkey-Turkey knew when he was outnumbered. He leaped back up the tree and took off, flying deeper into the woods.

'That's right!' Willow shouted. 'Fly away, fly away, fly away home!'

'And don'ts come back!' shouted Ogden.

'The Monster Mashers did it again!' cried Fenella. 'They saved the grannies!' She nodded to the villagers, and started to clap and cheer. The villagers joined in. 'Now, back to the village. There's some disco dancing that needs to be done!'

Everyone tidied up the wool, and started back towards the village, patting Ogden on the back. Even Angry Man looked happier.

As Willow picked up the boom box and the glitter ball, she realised that Jiggy was lagging behind. She went up to her. 'Don't worry, Jiggy. That turkey has gone for good. He won't be bothering us again.'

Jiggy shook her head. 'This dance isn't over, Willowtree. From one wise bird to another, that freaky fowl wanted something from us grannies. And he'll be back to get it, just you see.'

W hen they reached the village hall, everyone worked quickly to get into the disco mood. Ogden and Willow – and all of the rest of the dancers – quickly changed into their dance clothes, and the room was an array of glitter, sparkles and feathers, in all colours of the rainbow. The Big Disco Night trophy was polished, and the flashing lights were switched on. The hall looked incredible!

But as Willow was warming up, it was hard for her to concentrate. She kept thinking about what Jiggy had said. Would the Lurkey-Turkey really come back? Why had he taken the grannies in the first place? Willow didn't like an unsolved mystery. She tried to push her worries to the back of her head.

Everyone practised their disco moves while the band set up their instruments at one end of the hall. It was nearly time for the Big Disco Night to begin.

'Well done, Monster Mashers!' the Mayor said to Willow and Ogden. 'You got the grannies back, and the disco can now go ahead. We owe you so much.'

'That's what we're here for!' Willow

smiled, as she straightened Ogden's fuzzy pink wig, and wrapped his new gold-tipped feather boa around his neck. But secretly, she was still thinking about the Lurkey-Turkey. What did he want? It really made no sense at all.

'Hmm, this hall really is looking "super cool",' said the Mayor. 'All we need now is the glitter ball. Does anyone know where it is?'

'Oh!' Willow said. 'I left it on the step outside, with the balls of wool. I'll get it and then we can begin!' She quickly ran to the door, and stepped outside. The sun

was beginning to set, and Willow shivered in her thin disco clothes. She bent over to pick up the glitter ball, nestled amongst the wool. 'Balls of wool, that's so strange,' she said to herself. 'When the grannies were captured, they left behind knitting things.' She crouched down by the basket, and picked up one of the balls. 'Even Ogden had been washing woolly clothing when he was ogre-napped. And Jiggy was holding a thimble when she was taken. Knitting? Is that the connection?' Willow frowned.

'What does it mean?' she whispered to herself. 'Why would the Lurkey-Turkey care about knitting things?' She tossed the wool back into the basket, and picked up the glitter ball again. As she straightened up, she felt the ground shake.

Thud!
Thud! Thud!

Willow turned round slowly, holding the glitter ball in front of her.

'Gobble, gobble, gobble!
Gobble, gobble, gobble!'

There, standing on the path, his feathers fanned out around him, was the Lurkey-Turkey. He looked at Willow with his terrible eye, and stretched out a long, sharp claw towards her.

'Wha—?'

Before Willow had time to say anything, the Lurkey-Turkey had grabbed her and thrown her onto his back. He snatched the basket of wool in his beak and bounded down the path, Willow still holding the glitter ball with one hand and clinging to the turkey's thick, black feathers with the other. The Lurkey-Turkey jumped into the air, his huge wings beating fast, lifting them up into the sky.

Meanwhile, Ogden trotted out of the door in his platform boots. Why was Willow taking so long with the glitter ball? He wanted the disco to begin! He looked left and right, but couldn't see Willow anywhere. The glitter ball wasn't on the steps, and the wool had gone as well.

'Ogden!'

He heard a noise from above. There, fast disappearing into the distance, was Willow on the back of the Lurkey-Turkey!

He charged into the woods. The sun was fast disappearing, but the final rays of light reflected off the glitter ball and showed Ogden the way, like a shining star. Straightaway, Ogden knew where the Lurkey-Turkey was going: he was flying back to his nest.

Sure enough, the massive bird landed on top of the giant oak tree, and Willow slithered off his back into the nest.

Ogden reached the tree. He had to climb, and climb fast. He scaled the mighty oak, his fuzzy wig wobbling on his head as he stretched and pulled himself up.

Jumpety-bumpety, bump-bump-bump!

Wacka-wacka woo!
Wacka-wacka boogaloo!

'Happy sounds.' Ogden stopped climbing. He could hear the music playing from the village hall. The villagers had it turned up, full volume. He loved to listen to it, he could feel the tingling starting in his feet, feel the beat moving through his legs and arms, making him want to shake and shimmy and get lost in the wonderful jumpety-bumpety music . . .

'No!' he said to himself, firmly. 'Rescue Little Will, then disco. Dancing has to waits. Friends first.'

One hand after another, one

platform-booted left foot after another, he climbed again. Finally, he got to the top of the tree, and threw one leg over the side of the giant nest.

'Hello, Og,' whispered Willow. She was sitting in the middle of the nest, with the turkey perched on the other side of the nest, glowering at them both. Ogden pulled himself up, about to jump into the nest—

'No!' Willow held up her hand, and Ogden froze. 'Be carefully-careful, Og.' She pointed. All around her were six large, smooth eggs. Willow looked up at Ogden with a small smile. 'The Lurkey-Turkey brought me to see his babies.'

'**Gobble, gobble,**' said the turkey, softly. He bent down and picked up a ball of wool in his dribbly beak, and tossed it at Willow. She caught it in one hand.

'What . . .' Willow said to the turkey. 'What do you want me to do?'

The Lurkey-Turkey bent down and gently tapped one of the eggs with his beak. Then he reached over and picked up two small stick-like things and dropped them in Willow's lap. She picked them up.

'Knitting needles?'

'Gobble.' The turkey nodded, lightly tapping an egg again.

'Gobble, gobble, gobble!'

'Eggs gets cold when he's not here,' Ogden said. 'Turkey wants little coats for thems.'

'Ogden.' Willow looked aghast. 'I never knew you could talk turkey!'

Ogden shrugged an ogre-y shrug. 'You never asked.'

Willow pulled a face at him. 'So that's why he brought the grannies here, and that's why he took the wool. He wanted the grannies to knit him egg cosies!'

'**Gobble**.' The turkey nodded again, and a gloopy tear ran down from his one eye. '**Gobbly-gobble.**'

Ogden sighed. 'Turkey all alone. No ones to sit and warm the eggsies when he's away.'

Willow felt a lump in her throat. She sat up, and looked at the turkey. 'Don't worry,

Lurkey-Turkey. We will help you look after your babies. I'm not very good at knitting, but I know some grannies who are. We'll all go and ask them together.'

'Keeps these eggsies warms.' Ogden unwrapped his new feather boa from his neck, and tucked it round the eggs. He took his pink fuzzy wig off and put it on the biggest egg. 'Now, let's gets knitting!'

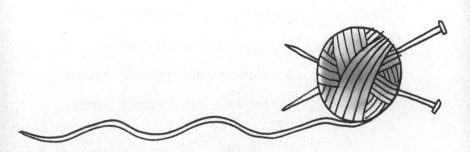

When Ogden, Willow and the Lurkey-Turkey got back to the village hall, the disco was in full swing. The jumpety-bumpety beat was pumping out, and through the windows they could see the multi-coloured lights that were flashing in time with the music.

'Disco fever.' Ogden murmured.

As he watched, Ogden's huge feet began to tap, his hairy shoulders began to shake, and his big behind jiggled in time to the music. Dozens of dancers were bustling across the floor to the disco beat, wearing dazzling clothes of every colour.

'Ooh, sparkles!' Ogden cooed.

There were dancers jumping up and down. There were dancers holding one another while they pranced about the room. There were people doing the **Mashed Potato,** the **Boogaloo,** the **Hustle,** and the **Shake.** Jiggy was **jiving,** Fenella was **freestyling.** Even the grannies were tap-tapping their feet.

'Did anyone even notice we were missing?' Willow said.

'Thems will notice now.' Ogden flung the door open, and stepped into the hall, followed by Willow and the Lurkey-Turkey.

'Stop the music!' shouted Willow. But nobody heard her.

'Stops the dancing!' called out Ogden. But nobody noticed him.

'**Gobble! Gobble!**' gobbled the Lurkey-Turkey. That got everyone's attention.

The music stopped, the dancing stopped, and the Mayor fell over in a dizzy swoon. Everyone shouted, 'Run for your lives!' and scurried around in circles, their arms in the air.

'Wait!' cried Willow. 'It's all OK! The turkey doesn't mean us any harm, he just needs our help!'

'Help! Help! Help!' everyone screamed.

Fenella froze, Jiggy jolted to a halt. But nobody else listened, they just ran around some more, until **SLAM!**

Jiggy stood at the closed door, face flushed purple. 'You better tell us why you've brought that turkey back, Willow and Ogden. And talk fast. Because nobody here wants to get gobble, gobble, gobbled.'

'You were right, Jiggy,' Willow said. 'The Lurkey-Turkey was looking for something. He was looking for our help.' She stepped forward. 'Ogden can understand the turkey, and he's told us everything. We saw the turkey's nest. He has six eggs – they're his babies – and no one to help him care for them. When he leaves his nest for food, the eggs get cold. If they get too cold, they won't hatch.' She walked up to the Lurkey-Turkey and put a comforting hand on his giant wing.

'Lurkey-Turkey needed the grannies to do something he couldn't do himself. To knit some woolly egg cosies for his babies. That's all. He didn't mean to scare anyone!'

'Are you sure?' The Mayor stood up, fanning himself with his hand. 'And when these baby turkeys hatch out, are they going to terrorise us all with their constant demands for knitted goods?'

'Gobble, gobble!' The Lurkey-Turkey shook his head. 'Gobble, gobble, gobble, gobbly-gob, gobble. Gob, Gobbly-gobble. Gobble gob-gob, gobbly gobble.'

'He said no,' said Ogden.

'There!' Willow said. 'So we just have to knit some cosies, and all will be well!'

'Did someone say "knitting"?' Granny Grunter stepped forward. 'We're the best knitters this side of the Purple Mountains.'

'Pah!' Granny Magee stood up. 'Best knitters in the kingdom!'

'Give me my needles!' declared Granny Smith.

'Has anyone got any biscuits?' said Granny Fuzzbun.

Willow gathered the wool, Fenella found knitting needles, and Freddo Fuzzbun opened a big tin of Crunchy-Crispy Disco Delights that the baker had made that morning.

'We need some tunes to get us in the groove!' cried Jiggy, and band started to play again. In no time the grannies were knitting up a storm, their needles going **clickety-click** in time to the disco beat. Ogden unravelled wool as he shimmied, Fenella nodded her head as she stitched the cosies up the sides wearing the lucky thimble, and Willow danced around the room, giving out biscuits to the hungry grannies. Even the Lurkey-Turkey wobbled his wattle and shook his feathery behind.

In no time, the grannies had knitted six beautiful and very warm-looking egg cosies: a stripy one, a spotty one, a zigzaggy cosy, a cosy with stars, a cosy with flowers and a cosy with a big smiley face on it.

'Gobble, gobble, gobble!' The Lurkey-Turkey looked very pleased indeed. He gathered the cosies carefully under his wing. 'Gobbly-gob gobble,' he said to Ogden. 'Gob, gob, gob.'

'Thanks, Lurkey-Turkey,' said Ogden.

'What did he say?' Willow whispered.

'He say to pay Og back he carry all them monsters in the jailhouse far-far away on his back tomorrow.'

'That's great!' said Willow. 'Who knows? Maybe he'll be a new recruit for the Monster Masher team!'

The two friends watched as Lurkey-Turkey waddled out of the doors and turned one last time to the grannies. 'Gobble, gobble!' He winked at them with his one googly eye, then flew off into the sunset.

'All this gobbling makes Og oh-so hungry,' Ogden said.

'No time for eating now, Ogden!' Willow said. 'We've got a disco trophy to win!'

'Before you do . . .' Fenella said, taking something from Granny Grunter. 'The grannies have knitted you something special to say thank you for rescuing them from the tree.' She held up some bright,

woollen things in each hand. 'Pink for you, Ogden. Blue for Willow. They're legwarmers! Perfect for all your disco dancing!'

'Oooh, super cool!' said Ogden, as he pulled on the sparkly legwarmers.

'No, Ogden, super warm!' Willow laughed, as she put hers on.

'Music, please!' Jiggy shouted. 'Let's do, do, do – do the Funky Chicken! Or should I say, the Lurkey-Turkey!'

'Gobble, gobble, gobble!' shouted Ogden.

He flapped his wings, and shook his tail feather.

'The Monster Mashers do it again!' the Mayor cried. 'Now where did we put that glitter ball?'

The music started once more, and Ogden strutted out onto the floor and danced round the room, twisting and twirling, stopping only to take Willow's and Jiggy's hands and spin them giggling across the hall in a blaze of rainbow colours.

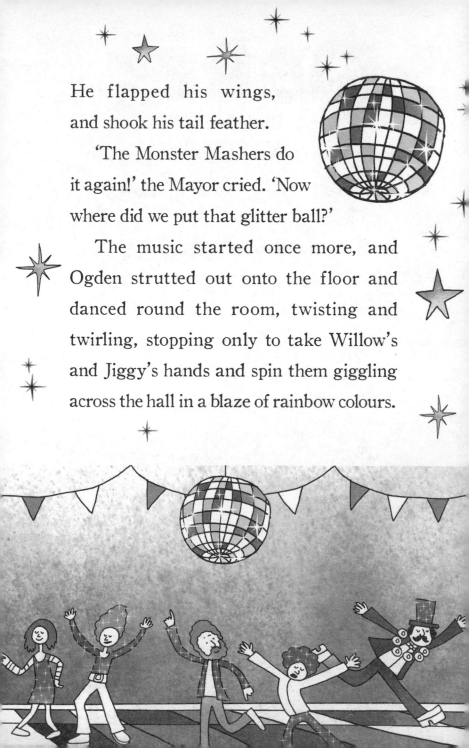

OGRES

Don't

DANCE

KIRSTY MCKAY

Illustrated by Chris Judge

What do you call a big, green, ugly ogre
who loves to dance?

A BOOGIEMAN!

Ogden is a foot-tapping,
man-eating ogre. He's got
two left feet but he still
loves to dance to the beat.
And now he's looking for
his perfect dance partner…

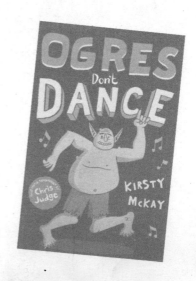

'Delightfully entertaining'
Lovereading

9781849397155   £4.99